THE
QUEEN'S KNICKERS

NICHOLAS ALLAN

Mini Treasures

RED FOX

To Jenny

1 3 5 7 9 10 8 6 4 2

Copyright © Nicholas Allan 1993

Nicholas Allan has asserted his right under the Copyright, Designs and Patents Act, 1988
to be identified as the author and illustrator of this work.

First published in the United Kingdom 1993 by Hutchinson Children's Books

First published in Mini Treasures edition 1998 by Red Fox
Random House, 20 Vauxhall Bridge Road, London, SW1V 2SA

Random House Australia (Pty) Ltd
20 Alfred Street, Milsons Point, Sydney, New South Wales 2061, Australia

Random House New Zealand Limited
18 Poland Road, Glenfield,
Auckland 10, New Zealand

Random House South Africa
PO Box 2263, Rosebank 2121, South Africa

RANDOM HOUSE UK Limited Reg No. 954009

A CIP catalogue record for this book is available from the British library.

ISBN 0 099 26356 4

Printed in Singapore

The Queen likes to dress smartly.

So she has an enormous wardrobe
for her clothes...

...and a slightly smaller chest of drawers
for all her knickers.

Dilys looks after the Queen's knickers.

She has a special trunk for when the Queen goes away.

One day the trunk went *missing*!

It caused a great crisis...

...and was only just sorted out before it reached
the NEWS AT TEN.

The trunk had got mixed up...

...with a picnic hamper.

ROYAL WEDDINGS

STATE FUNERALS

HORSE RIDING
(WITH EXTRA PADDING)

FOREIGN VISITS

The Queen has knickers

KNICKER GUIDE

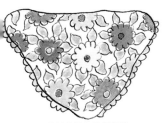

GARDEN PARTIES

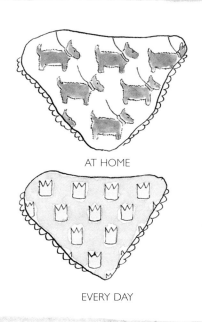

AT HOME

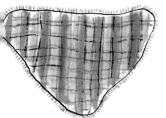

BALMORAL (WOOLLEN)

EVERY DAY

or all occasions.

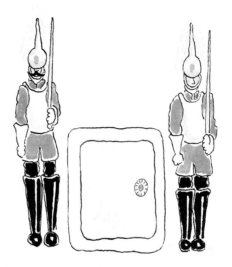

At the opening of Parliament the Queen
wears her VIP's (Very Important Pair).
There is no picture of these. But here is
the safe where they're locked up with
other state secrets.

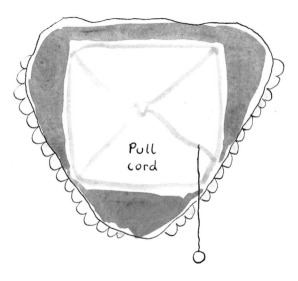

When she travels she has special
knickers with a small parachute
inside them...

...just in case.

(She has another pair for

hen she's on board ship.)

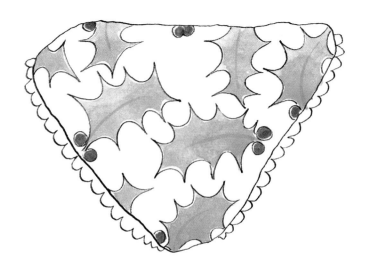

But her most special knickers are her
Christmas knickers. They are a gift from
Scandinavia and are traditionally
decorated with real holly...

...which is why
she keeps her Christmas
message very short.

The Royal Knickers, though, are her most
valuable. They are made of pure silk
with gold thread and encrusted with
diamonds, emeralds, and rubies.

They were first worn by Queen
Victoria and are rather baggy.

I wonder what knickers the
Queen would wear
if she visited our school?

There'd be a *terrific* flap at the Palace.

'Call the Royal Knicker-maker, Dilys!'

'Oh no! Far too fancy!'

'Oh no! Far too frilly!'

'Oh no! Far too plain!'

'Oh no! Far too ... SILLY!'

'I shall just have to wear my "Every Day" knickers.'

Then the poor Queen would feel very awkward,
as she's so particular about her clothes.

But I would tell her something to put her at ease.
'Don't worry about your knickers,
Your Majesty,' I'd whisper.
'You see, *no one can see them anyway*.'

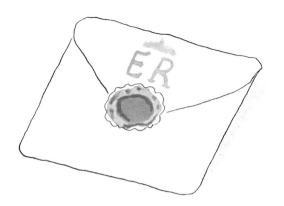

Then she'd be sure to send a special note
to me afterwards by the Royal Mail saying:

'Her majesty wishes
to inform you that her
visit was most enjoyable...
and very comfortable.'